Five Little Monkeys Jumping on the Bed

Retold and Illustrated by

EILEEN CHRISTELOW

SCHOLASTIC INC.

New York Toronto London Auckland Sydney
Mexico City New Delhi Hong Kong

For

Heather   Morgan

Joni

Grady   Stefan

———————————————————

ISBN 0-590-99459-X

24 23 22   1/0

Printed in the U.S.A.

It was bedtime. So five little monkeys took a bath.

Five little monkeys put on their pajamas.

Five little monkeys brushed their teeth.

Five little monkeys said good night to their mama.

Then...five little monkeys jumped on the bed!

One fell off and bumped his head.

The mama called the doctor. The doctor said,

"No more monkeys jumping on the bed!"

So four little monkeys...

...jumped on the bed.

One fell off and bumped his head.

The mama called the doctor.　　The doctor said,

"No more monkeys jumping on the bed!"

So three little monkeys jumped on the bed.

One fell off and bumped her head.

The mama called the doctor. The doctor said,

"No more monkeys jumping on the bed!"

So two little monkeys jumped on the bed.

One fell off and bumped his head.

The mama called the doctor.

The doctor said,

"No more monkeys jumping on the bed!"

So one little monkey jumped on the bed.

She fell off and bumped her head.

The mama called the doctor.

The doctor said,

"NO MORE MONKEYS JUMPING ON THE BED!"

So five little monkeys fell fast asleep.

"Thank goodness!" said the mama.

"Now I can go to bed!"